My Little Pony™
and the New Friends

by Edith Adams
illustrated by Cathy Beylon

RANDOM HOUSE 🏠 NEW YORK

Every morning when it was sunny the Little Ponies trotted from their stable to the beach. There they played on the sand and splashed in the waves. Firefly and Medley liked to fly along the water's edge.

On the beach were some big rocks. This was the Little Ponies' favorite place. Applejack liked to lie on the rocks and watch the fish in the pools. And when the sun was high the Little Ponies rested in the shadow of the rocks.

One day when the Little Ponies went down to the beach they found a surprise. There, playing on their favorite rocks, were two children!

"Let's make friends with them," said Applejack. "Children are fun to play with, and they often have good things to eat."

"No, no!" said Firefly. "Children are nasty. A child once threw a stone at me while I was flying. I don't like them."

"These children look kind," said Blossom. "Come on, Firefly, let's make friends with them."

But Firefly would not. The ponies trotted toward the children, and Firefly flew off alone.

The children and the Little Ponies had lots of fun. They ran races and played tag. Medley gave the children rides, and at lunchtime the children shared their lunch with the ponies.

"Tomorrow we will bring you some special treats," said the girl.

That night, when the Little Ponies were back in their cozy stable, they talked about all the fun they had had that day.

"Come with us tomorrow, Firefly," said Medley. "Then we can both give them rides."

"No!" said Firefly. "Children are nasty."

The next day the Little Ponies played with the children again. But Firefly stayed away. She rolled in the sand and splashed in the water, but after a while she got lonely. She flew over the spot where the Little Ponies and the children were playing. "It does look like they're having fun," she thought.

But when she heard the boy call, "Firefly, please come and play with us," she pretended not to hear.

Firefly flew far out to sea. "Humph," she said to herself. "I can have fun without children." And she did a double flip to prove it. Then she saw a school of dolphins and some whales, so she dived down to take a closer look.

Firefly was so busy watching the whales and dolphins that she didn't notice the dark clouds gathering in the sky. Suddenly there was a flash of lightning and it began to rain—hard!

"I must get back to shore!" thought Firefly as the rain came pouring down. Soon her wings were soaked through. They got so heavy that Firefly could hardly move them. She began to fall.

Suddenly—splash! Firefly was in the water. "I hope I can swim to the shore," she said, out of breath, as a huge wave crashed over her head.

Back on the shore the Little Ponies and the children had seen Firefly fall into the water.

"We must do something!" said the girl. "Medley, please help us!"

"Of course I will!" said Medley.

The boy ran to fetch a rope. Then he and the girl quickly climbed on to Medley's back.

Firefly was struggling in the water. She was so tired she could hardly swim.

Just then she heard the girl shout, "Firefly, catch this! Catch this rope! We'll pull you to shore." The girl threw the rope—and Firefly caught it!

At last Firefly reached the shore. She struggled out of the water and lay panting on the sand. All the Little Ponies crowded around her.

"Oh, Firefly, we thought you would never get back," said Blossom.

"I wouldn't have," said Firefly, "without help from the children and Medley." She gave a little nicker. "Thank you," she said to the children.

The next day Firefly and the other Little Ponies played with the children. Firefly had lots of fun, and as a special thank-you to her new friends, she took them flying high above the sea.